# Muktar WITHDRAWN
## and the
# Camels

**JANET GRABER**

illustrated by **SCOTT MACK**

Christy Ottaviano Books
Henry Holt and Company
New York

For Hannah Grace and
Caroline Anne, with special love,
and for all the children of Somalia:
Let there be peace.
                    —J. G.

Special thanks to Janet Graber and Christy Ottaviano
for giving me the opportunity to put Janet's story
into pictures. Thanks also for the continuous love and
inspiration from Laurie, my parents, and my family.
                    —S. M.

Henry Holt and Company, LLC, *Publishers since 1866*
175 Fifth Avenue, New York, New York 10010
www.HenryHoltKids.com

Henry Holt® is a registered trademark of Henry Holt and Company, LLC.
Text copyright © 2009 by Janet Graber
Illustrations copyright © 2009 by Scott Mack
All rights reserved.
Distributed in Canada by H. B. Fenn and Company Ltd.

Library of Congress Cataloging-in-Publication Data
Graber, Janet.
Muktar and the camels / Janet Graber ; illustrated by Scott Mack. – 1st ed.
    p.        cm.
"Christy Ottaviano Books."
Summary: Muktar, an eleven-year-old refugee living in a Kenyan orphanage, dreams of tending camels again, as he did with his
nomadic family in Somalia, and has a chance to prove himself when a traveling librarian with an injured camel arrives at his school.
ISBN-13: 978-0-8050-7834-3 / ISBN-10: 0-8050-7834-7
[1. Orphans–Fiction. 2. Refugees–Fiction. 3. Camels–Fiction. 4. Schools–Fiction. 5. Somalis–Kenya–Fiction.
6. Kenya–Fiction.] I. Mack, Scott, ill. II. Title.
PZ7.G7488Muk 2009 [Fic]–dc22 2008038217

First Edition–2009 / Designed by Elynn Cohen
The artist used oils on canvas to create the illustrations for this book.
Printed in China on acid-free paper. ∞

10  9  8  7  6  5  4  3  2  1

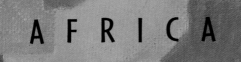

A F R I C A

KENYA

SOMALIA

**B**are feet slap across the hard earthen floor of the Iftin Orphanage as children gather in the dining hall to gobble down bowls of warm *posho*.

Sweet-smelling steam rises from Muktar's bowl and tickles his nose.

"Eat up, lazy fellow," calls Mr. Hassan, their teacher.

But Muktar gazes out the window, across the dusty landscape. He remembers a time before drought and war engulfed his homeland. A time when his family roamed Somalia, their worldly possessions strapped to mighty camels.

Muktar had gathered camel dung to fuel campfires.
His mother beat thick sour camel milk into cheese, spun
camel hair into thread, wove the thread into clothing. Over
and over his father said, *Camels first. Always camels first.*
*Camels are treasure.*

"Stop daydreaming, lazy fellow!" Mr. Hassan claps his hands.

"Don't cause trouble," whispers Muktar's best friend, Ismail.

Muktar stirs his *posho* with sticky fingers. "My mother and father rest in graves beneath piles of stones." He scoops the porridge into his mouth. "I miss my parents. I miss wandering." He stares at the acacia trees dotting the scrubby land. "And I miss camels."

"The world has changed," says Ismail. "I will learn the new ways."

"Pah! How can you? There are no books."

"Silence, Muktar," calls Mr. Hassan. "Time for class."

The children follow Mr. Hassan into the dusty courtyard and squat in shadows cast by the sun-baked walls. Mr. Hassan scratches squiggly letters on a blackboard.

A dry wind ripples rivulets of sand over Muktar's toes. Words hum and buzz in his head like a swarm of bees. Muktar fingers the gnarled root he keeps in the pocket of his shorts. *Take it, Muktar*, his father whispered before he died. *Use it wisely.*

The root is all Muktar has left of the old ways.

A blazing sun beats down. Muktar's eyelids droop. He dozes.

Muktar dreams of a large camel, its brown eyes fringed with double lashes. He brushes dust and mud from its shaggy coat. He slips a sugar lump between its lips, tough as elephant hide.

He climbs up behind the hump and feels the camel's rear legs rising, pitching him forward, forward, forward . . .

*Chunk, chunk, chunk,* wooden
bells clang and clank.
*Phut, phut, phut,* giant feet
whisper in the sand.

Muktar stirs and opens his eyes. Three camels, tail to
bridle, lope through the thickets toward the courtyard.

"Greetings," calls the driver, next to Number One camel. "I am Bisharm Mohamed, librarian, bringing you books from Garissa."

"Camels!" gasps Muktar.

"Books," breathes Ismail.

"A miracle!" shouts Mr. Hassan, clapping his hands.

Number Two camel carries steel poles, tarps, and woven mats. Number Three camel bears wooden boxes, slung on either side of her hump. The children flock around the camels like fluttering hoopoe birds. "Order. Order. Sit immediately!" shouts Mr. Hassan. "Ismail. Muktar. You are the eldest. Help Mr. Mohamed."

Shivers of delight skip down Muktar's spine. He savors the sour smell of the camels as he prods tent poles into the hard ground. Mr. Mohamed ties tarps. Ismail lays scarlet and gold mats beneath the awning.

"Unload the books," says Mr. Mohamed. "Spit-spot!"

Muktar strokes the shaggy hair of Number Three camel. *Ssh, ssh, ssh*, he orders. The camel dips her great head and sinks to her knees with a groan. Muktar frowns. Number Three camel has a deep cut in one of the two fleshy pads of her right forefoot. "Please, sir—"

"Hurry, boys, hurry," shouts Mr. Mohamed. "No time to waste."

Soon there are piles of books scattered all over the woven mats.

"Muktar, guard these cantankerous beasts while I supervise the library."

"But, Mr. Mohamed sir, Number Three camel—"

"Not now, boy. I am very busy."

But how can Mr. Mohamed return to Garissa with an injured camel?
Muktar frets. *Camels first. Always camels first.* His father's golden rule.

*Ush, ush, ush.* The camels follow Muktar. They slurp cool water at the
pump. Muktar fills a bucket and leads them to the edge of the courtyard.
The camels graze on a thicket of thornbushes.

Muktar rubs his hands down the spindly leg of the hurt camel. She growls deep in her throat and nips Muktar's arm. *Ssh, ssh, ssh*, he mutters. The camel drops onto her knobby knees. He splashes water over the deep gash in her pad. "Cut on a rock," Muktar whispers, caressing her long nose.

Muktar pulls out the twisted root from inside his pocket.

He bites off a piece and chews and chews. When his mouth is filled with paste, he spits the tart mush into the camel's wound.

Then he removes his shirt, tears it into strips, and binds the giant two-toed foot.

"All better," Muktar hums into the camel's furry ear.

Bowls clatter in the dining hall. Idle chatter drifts through the windows. Muktar smells *matoke*. His favorite meal. How his stomach rumbles for steamed banana! But he is responsible for the camels.

The immense animals rest in the shade of the thornbushes, chewing on cud. They belch and grunt. Muktar sprawls in the shade of their heaving bellies. The tangy smell of fresh excrement makes him drowsy.

He dreams he is collecting dung for the cooking fire once more. He dreams that his mother's simmering pot fills the encampment with the rich smell of spicy stew. He dreams of sleeping on a mat of straw beneath the stars.

"Wake up, lazy fellow. Wake up!" Mr. Hassan shakes Muktar's shoulder.
Muktar rubs his eyes.

"Time for me to go," shouts Mr. Mohamed, striding across the courtyard.

Muktar scrambles to his feet. "Please, sir, Number Three camel injured her foot."

"Pish-posh!" Mr. Mohamed slaps his thigh. "What am I to do?"

"I tried to tell you," Muktar mumbles.

"What good is that to me now?" Mr. Mohamed scowls.

"Please, sir, it is fixed." Muktar points to the bandaged foot.

"He knows camels," explains Mr. Hassan. "He's a nomad."

"How old are you, boy?" asks Mr. Mohamed.

"Almost twelve years, sir."

"Trustworthy?"

"He's a decent fellow," says Mr. Hassan. "Bit of a dreamer."

"Is that so, Muktar?" Mr. Mohamed stares. "And what do you dream?"

Muktar's heart misses a beat. No one has ever asked him such a question.

He crimps his fingers into the coils of coarse brown hair on Number Three's neck. He dreams of treasuring camels like his father, and his grandfather, and his great-grandfather, back through all the generations of the Somali people.

"Please, sir." He tugs the librarian's arm. "I wish to tend camels."

"Do you now?" Mr. Mohamed smiles.

Muktar nods.

"Mr. Hassan, I need an assistant," says Mr. Mohamed. "Someone to care for these ornery beasts. Someone like this boy. Myself, I'd rather drive a truck, but trucks are useless in the desert!"

Muktar longs to ride again. To feel a camel beneath him unfolding and stretching and gliding across the sand. He holds his breath.

"Take him, dear fellow, take him." Mr. Hassan claps his hands.

Muktar leans into the camel's belly.

Ismail pads across the courtyard with a plate of *matoke*.

"I am to care for the camels!" Muktar whoops.

"I shall miss you, my friend," says Ismail, offering the fragrant fruit.

"And I you." Muktar slips morsels of sweet banana into his mouth.

"But I can visit you each time I bring books to the orphanage."

"Yes, indeed," says Ismail. "With books I will learn to be a teacher.
Books delivered by Muktar and the camels."
Muktar claps his hands. "Not a lazy fellow anymore!"

# Author's Note

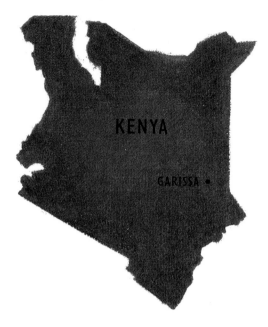

KENYA

GARISSA •

In the last years of the twentieth century, the country of Somalia was devastated by drought, famine, and a vicious civil war. Thousands of Somali nomads fled for their lives, and camps and orphanages sprang up along the border between Kenya and Somalia.

PHOTO BY CHLOÉ/GALBE.COM

Garissa is a dusty enclave of 200,000 people in Kenya's North Eastern Province. From Garissa, the Kenya National Library Service dispatches a three-camel convoy eight times a month to deliver books to schools and orphanages in the hinterlands, where bandits roam and roads are few.